The Jewish Mother Goose

The Jewish Mother Goose

Modified Rhymes for Meshugennah Times

By David Borgenicht

RUNNING PRESS
PHILADELPHIA · LONDON

9 8 7 6 5 4 3 2 1
Digit on the right indicates the number of this printing

Library of Congress Cataloging-in-Publication Number 99-74347

ISBN 0-7624-0675-5

Cover and interior illustrations by Bethann Thornburgh
Cover and interior design by Terry Peterson
Typography: Goudy Old Style, Habitat, Mead, Spectrum, Stone Sans, Stone Serif, and Weisbaden

This book may be ordered by mail from the publisher. Please include $2.50 for postage and handling.
But try your bookstore first!

Running Press Book Publishers
125 South Twenty-second Street
Philadelphia, Pennsylvania 19103-4399

Visit us on the web!
www.runningpress.com

De Taybel of Kontentz

Acknowligmentz

I am truly gebentsht to have had such wonderful support from a variety of sources in making this book happen. Many thanks and a big plate of schnecken go to: Nancy Borgenicht and Louis Borgenicht (who gave me the best reformed Jewish education a boychik could have); Helen and Wally Sandack (for writing those "Temple Follies" so many years ago; see also "De Entroduction"); Rabbi Silver (who bar mitsvahed me); Congregation Kol Ami; Camp Shwayder and Camp Swig; Leo Rosten (for *The Joys of Yiddish* and *The Education of Hyman Kaplan*); and of course, David Smith (my agent) and Caroline Tiger (my editor). Mazel Tov!

De Entroduction

The Jewish Mother Goose: An Explanation

This collection of poems is just a big joke
So don't get all miffed at the fun that I poke.

And don't worry too much that I'm stereotyping
I'm Jewish myself—enough with the griping.

They're just little verses I made up at night
They're not generalizations, there's no wrong or right.

Just read and enjoy them—there's no need to fret.
Besides, it's my family who should be upset.

I have no idea where this book came from. Yes, I am Jewish and yes, my family is Jewish (even though we all come from Utah, which is another story altogether). Yes, I am a writer, of sorts. And yes, I fondly remember my childhood nursery rhymes.

But I never planned to write the poems you hold in front of you at this very moment. They just arrived. Like Wee Willie Weinstein, they appeared out of nowhere. The Jewish muse struck, and I couldn't get her to stop kvetching.

In retrospect, I can justify it. I can tell you why this book should exist—in fact, I can tell you four good reasons:

1) To continue and preserve the ancient art of Jewish literary humor. (Some may question the use of the word "literary," but hey, the book's got words, right?)

2) To teach new generations a lot of funny Yiddish words that are in danger of disappearing. (How many other books, excluding *The Joys of Yiddish*, let you see "nudnik," "macher," and "kishka," all in one place?)

3) To allow us to laugh at each other, and at ourselves. (The key, I'm convinced, to survival, as well as all success and joy in life.)

4) To bring about world peace. (A bit of a stretch, I admit, but maybe if everyone put aside their differences and arguments and guns and took some time to read a few funny books, we could get there.)

But none of that entered my mind at the moment my muse marched in through the front door, like Elijah. What entered my mind was this:

Little boy Lou! Go get your stuff!
Your father's in Scarsdale waiting for us!

It just grew from there—and more than fifty poems later, *The Jewish Mother Goose* was born.

I couldn't have written this book without the help of my grandfather, A. Wally Sandack. Not only did he give me (I mean loan me—don't worry, Grandpa) his precious copies of Leo Rosten's *The Joys of Yiddish* and Harry Golden's *Only in America*, as well as his prized possession, Milt Gross's incredible "Hiawatta" ("On de shurrs from Geetchy Goony/Stoot a tipee witt a weegwom"), he gave me something much more important.

He taught me how to embrace life. How to work hard, how to laugh every day. How to enjoy Walter Matthau and Mickey Katz. How to make a great kosher hot dog. How to love who we are. How to make a funny face. How to tell a great joke, or even a bad one ("Sandack! Come home!"). And perhaps most importantly, how to speak with a Yiddish accent. (By the way, you'll enjoy the book much more if you read it out loud with a Yiddish or New York Jewish accent.)

So actually, in hindsight, maybe that's where this book came from. From Grandpa Wally. After all, I couldn't have written it without him.

And if you like it, if you laugh a bit, you've got Grandpa Wally to thank.

I know I do.

Two notes about the contentz: 1) The titles of the original Mother Goose rhymes appear in parentheses beneath each Jewish Mother Goose title. 2) "De Glussary" (see page 91) will provide you with definitions and pronunciation guidelines.

De Pomes

Little Boy Lou

(Little Boy Blue)

Little boy Lou! Go get your stuff!
Your father's in Scarsdale waiting for us!

What? You're not wearing a coat? Are you crazy?
Are you stupid? Do you want to catch cold? Are you lazy?

Where's the nice coat Nana bought you last year?
You lost it at school? Oy gevalt—oy vay iz meer!

When I catch you, young Louis, your life won't be cushy.
I promise I'll smack you right there on your tushie.

Jack, Be Careful

(Jack Be Nimble)

Jack, be careful!
Jack, don't trip!
And wear a hat so you don't get sick.

There Was an Old Woman Who Lived in a Loafer

(There Was an Old Woman Who Lived in a Shoe)

There was an old woman who lived in a loafer.
She had fifty-five kids—but not one would come over!

She used all her powers of guilt when she called them,
But the kids just ignored her, her shoe just appalled them.

"They don't call, they don't write—why, not one comes to see me!"
But they'd never show up 'cause her house was so teeny!

So they pooled all their money and bought her a boot.
Size eleven, in leather—now ain't that a hoot?

And now the kids visit her every Shabbat.
But she still isn't happy—she now wants a yacht.

As I Was Going to Palm Springs

(As I Was Going to St. Ives)

As I was going to Palm Springs
(Where they have stores with gorgeous things),

I met a man who owned six condos—
Three in Rancho, three in Tahoe.

Every house had six jacuzzis.
Each jacuzzi had six blond floozies.

With condos, jacuzzis, and all the blond floozies,
Who can afford to live in Palm Springs?

To Macy's, To Macy's

(To Market, To Market)

To Macy's, to Macy's
To buy a new mixer.

That son of mine's going to marry a shiksa!

To MOMA, to MOMA
To buy him a card.

What? Would a nice Jewish girl be so hard?

To Zabar's, to Zabar's
To get me some sugar.

My friends will all think that my son is meshuggah!

To Fine and Shapiro
To buy me some bread.

Don't worry—I'm fine. I'd be better off dead.

Hush-a-Bye Bubbi

(Rock-a-bye Baby)

Hush-a-Bye Bubbi
In our guest room,
It's been three weeks now—
Are you leaving us soon?
We'll miss all your kvetching
And carrying on,
But please—
Won't you go back
To Boca Raton?

Applecake

(Pat-a-Cake)

Applecake, applecake,
Got it from the deli.
Also got gefilte—now
That ought to fill your belly.

Slice it up and squish it,
And mark it with a *B*
For your cousin Bernie—
It's his anniversary!

Brooklyn Bridge

(London Bridge)

Brooklyn Bridge is all backed up,
All backed up,
All backed up.
Brooklyn Bridge is all backed up,
I hate traffic!

Solomon Grumpy

(Solomon Grundy)

Solomon Grumpy
Fartoosht on Monday
Kvetching on Tuesday
Farmisht on Wednesday
Farchacda on Thursday
Meshugge on Friday
A klutz on Saturday
A pisher on Sunday
This is the life
Of Solomon Grumpy.

The Jewish Mother Goose

Old Sy Cohen

(Old King Cole)

Old Sy Cohen
Didn't know where he was goin',
But a happy old klutz was he.

He went wherever
The wind was a' blowin',
And then he walked into a tree.

Lillian Ruckus

(Little Miss Muffett)

Lillian Ruckus
Sat on her tucchis
Eating some bagels and lox.
Along came a goy
(Who played Lil like a toy)
And told her that she was a fox!

Lillian Ruckus
Got up off her tucchis
And bought the young goy some knishes.
This moral is real: When you need a good meal
Lil will get you whatever your wish is!

Hector Schecter, Big Hollywood Director

(Hector Protector)

Hector Schecter was dressed in Armani,
(The hotshot director once had lots of money).

Hector Schecter went over to Fox
To meet a producer who didn't wear socks.

He needed cash bad for his next big production,
(And he needed cash bad for his wife's liposuction).

But Hector's last movie was not a big hit
So no more Armanis for Hector—that's it!

Sing a Song of Shnecken

(Sing a Song of Sixpence)

Sing a song of shnecken—
Baked on Second Ave.,
It's the greatest shnecken
You'll ever have!

When the baking's over,
The register will ring.
"Eat your shnecken, Hon,"
The waitresses will sing.

Three Nice Guys

(Three Blind Mice)

Three nice guys,
Three nice guys,
See how they look?
See how they look?
They all went off to medical school,
They drive fancy cars and they all go to shul.
So why can't you be more like them, you big shmul!
Those three nice guys,
Three nice guys.

Hickory Dickory Doc-tor

(Hickory Dickory Dock)

Hickory Dickory Doc-tor
My head is completely farchacda!
My back hurts me too,
So what should I do,
My Hickory Dickory Doc-tor?

Take it easy for one day or two.
And don't give yourself too much to do.
Make some nice chicken soup,
And don't bend or stoop,
And by Thursday you'll feel good as new!

Three Wise Men of Great Neck

(Three Wise Men of Gotham)

Three wise men of Great Neck
Rode to work in a cab.
If the driver spoke English
I'd have words to sing with.

My Mother Ruth

(Old Mother Goose)

My mother Ruth,
When she traveled uptown,
Would make her poor children
Drive her around.

Larry, Larry Quite Contrary

(Mary, Mary Quite Contrary)

Larry! Why be so contrary?
Listen to what I'm telling.
I think what you're doing is wonderful.
My goodness! I'm practically kvelling!

You're no alter kocker,
In fact, you're a macher,
And I couldn't be more impressed.
You make a nice living, you're gentle and giving—
Now if only you knew how to dress.

If Wishes Were Knishes

(If Wishes Were Horses)

If wishes were knishes,
I'd never go hungry.

If husbands were maids,
I'd never do laundry.

And if "ifs" and "ands"
Were helping hands,
There'd be no work for lawyers.

Little Mo Green

(Little Bo Peep)

Little Mo Green just about burst his spleen
When his mother showed up at his door.
"My boychik! My Mo! I've got nowhere to go,
And I'm staying for two months or more!"

Little Mo Green took a shot of Jim Beam,
And said, "Mother, what a surprise!
I once heard you say you were coming in May,
And I just don't believe my own eyes."

Little Mo Green polished off his Jim Beam
And said "Mom, you know that I'm busy.
I've got lots to do—my taxes are due
And I don't want to get in a tizzy."

Mo Green's kind mother (who looked like Mo's brother)
Explained, "You won't know that I'm here.
I'll be helpful and quiet, and won't cause a riot.
And I see you but six times a year!"

This Is the House that Jack Bought

(This Is the House that Jack Built)

This is the house that Jack bought.

This is the carpet
That lays in the house that Jack bought.

This is the decorator
Who selected the carpet
That lays in the house that Jack bought.

This is the bill
That lists all the fixtures
That were picked by the decorator
Who selected the carpet
That lays in the house that Jack bought.

This is the expression
That goes on Jack's face
When Jack opens the bill
That lists all the fixtures
That were picked by the decorator
Who selected the carpet
That lays in the house that Jack bought.

Mr. Katz, Mr. Katz

(Pussycat, Pussycat)

"Mr. Katz! Mr. Katz!
Where have you been?"

"I've been with my family
Over in Queens."

"Mr. Katz! Mr. Katz!
What did you do there?"

"Felt guilty, annoyed,
and I lost some more hair!"

Benjy Boyer

(Simple Simon)

Benjy Boyer met a lawyer
Riding on the train.
Says Benjy Boyer to the lawyer,
"Can you save me pain?"

Says the lawyer to Benjy Boyer,
"First, I will need a down payment."
Says Benjy Boyer to the lawyer,
"You want I should live on the pavement?"

Peter Pepper

(Peter Piper)

Peter Pepper picked a peckel of pickled pickles.
A peckel of pickled pickles did Peter Pepper pick.
If Peter Pepper picked a peckel of pickled pickles,
What did he do with the money I gave him?

Jack Pratt

(Jack Sprat)

Jack Pratt
Can eat no fat,
(He's had a little scare.)

His wife
Is on a diet, too—
So all their shelves are bare.

Humpty Dumpy

(Humpty Dumpty)

Humpty Dumpy sat irked in his chair,
Humpty's wife Ethyl was doing her hair.

They were two hours late—they had tickets to *Rent*.
Oh, poor Humpty Dumpy—his patience was spent!

Not one of the very best counselors in town,
Could help out poor Humpty—he had a breakdown.

Doctor Fisher

(Doctor Foster)

Doctor Fisher, what a pisher!
Told me I was fat.
I said, "Go look in the mirror, Doc—
I mean, you're no Jack Sprat."

Rain, Rain

(Rain, Rain Go Away)

Rain, rain
My back's in pain—
Of course, I don't mean to complain.

I'll Tell You a Story

(I'll Tell You a Story)

I'll tell you a story about
Mildred Cory,
And now my story's begun.
She's having a fling
With a trainer named Bing,
And now my story is done.

Georgy Pierogie

(Georgy Porgy)

Georgy Pierogie, kugel and cake,
Kissed the goyls and made them quake.
"What a mensch!" the goyls all spake,
So they made young Georgy kugel and cake.

Wee Willie Weinstein

(Wee Willie Winkie)

Wee Willie Weinstein
Ran around the town,
East side, west side for his wife's nightgown.

Stopping in at Bloomies,
Shopping o'er at Saks,
"Do you have a present for my wife?" he'd always ask.

But Wee Willie Weinstein
Couldn't find a thing.
Next year he'd better start his shopping in the spring.

Mary Made a Roasted Lamb

(Mary Had a Little Lamb)

Mary made a roasted lamb,
Roasted lamb,
Roasted lamb.
Mary made a roasted lamb
For Passover night.

Everyone that came to her,
Came to her,
Came to her.
Everyone that came to her,
Found the meat just right.

"The secret to the recipe,
Recipe,
Recipe.
The secret to the recipe,
Is in the marinade.

"Soak it in some rosemary,
Rosemary,
Rosemary.
Soak it in some rosemary,
And kosher lemonade!"

Lucy Pollack
(Lucy Locket)

Lucy Pollack lost her wallet,
Kitty Cohen found it.
But nothing was inside so why'd
She make such fuss around it?

There Was an Old Man
(There Was an Old Man)

There was an old man,
Lived under a deli.
And if he's not gone,
He sure must be smelly.

Old Mother Lansky

(Old Mother Hubbard)

Old Mother Lansky
Went to the pantry,
To make her poor son some food.
But when she got there
Her pantry was bare,
And poor Mother Lansky felt rude!

So she schlepped herself over
To Buckman and Clover's,
Whose baked goods and meats were top-shelf.
They were so good, in fact,
By the time she came back,
She had eaten the food by herself!

59

Doctor Macher

(Doctor Fell)

I don't like you, Doctor Macher,
Even though you're quite a talker.
But I think you're off your rocker.
I don't like you, Doctor Macher.

Tweedle-Dork and Tweedle-Putz

(Tweedledum and Tweedledee)

Tweedle-Dork and Tweedle-Putz
Were having a discussion.
Then Tweedle-Dork hit Tweedle-Putz
And gave him a concussion.

Tweedle-Dork felt awful—
But he knew just what to do.
Tweedle-Dork hit Putz again
And said, "Now you've got two!"

Baa, Baa Black Sheep

(Baa, Baa Black Sheep)

Baa, baa black sheep
Have you any wool?
"Yes, but I need it
Or I'll be too cool.

"If I give my wool up
Sure, you'll have a sweater,
But I'll freeze my pupik off
When there's nasty weather."

The Little Girl with the Curl

(The Little Girl with the Curl)

There was a little girl,
Who had a little curl,
Right in the middle of her forehead.
When she made kishka it was very very good,
But when she made brisket it was horrid.

The Katzes of Kilkenny

(The Cats of Kilkenny)

Two Katzes lived right in Kilkenny.
Both thought there was one Katz too many.
So they kvetched and complained,
Drove each other insane,
'Til the both of them moved to South Denny.

A Week of Birthdays

(A Week of Birthdays)

Monday's child is quite a shlemiel.
Tuesday's child knows how to give shpiel.
Wednesday's child has lots of chutzpah,
Thursday's child is some good-looker,
Friday's child thinks he's a mensch,
Saturday's child emits a stench,
But the child that's born
On Sunday's fine.
She's perfect—just because she's mine.

Bagels with Cream Cheese

(Coffee and Tea)

Molly, my sister, and I fell out,
And what do you think it was all about?
She'd only eat a bagel when plain.
I shmeared hers with cream cheese,
And that caused her pain.

New Rochelle

(Banbury Cross)

Let's take a ride into New Rochelle,
To see your great aunt (who's not doing so well).
She thinks she's been living for years now, in France.
But that can't explain why she doesn't wear pants.

Tom, Tom the Butcher's Son

(Tom, Tom the Piper's Son)

Tom, Tom the butcher's son,
Stole a pig and away he run.
But the pig was traif,
So Tom, the naif
Gave it to the goyim to keep it safe.

The Ten O'Clock Caller

(The Ten O'Clock Scholar)

"A diller, a dollar, a ten o'clock caller!
Why must you call me so late?"

"Because, my dear mother,
If I called at another
Time, I'd not get a good rate!"

Peter Heller, Pickle Seller

(Peter Peter, Pumpkin Eater)

Peter Heller, pickle seller
Ran his business from the cellar.
But he's out of work today,
A flood took all his goods away.

Diddle Diddle Dumbkopf

(Diddle Diddle Dumpling)

Diddle diddle dumbkopf, my son John
Sleeps all day and at night he's gone!
He's a gonif, a nudnik—don't make me go on!
Diddle diddle dumbkopf, my son John.

Ladybug, Ladybug

(Ladybird, Ladybird)

Ladybug, ladybug
Why not stay home?
Your house is now empty, your children are gone.
"All but one child, and his name is Murray,
He just left his wife and he's coming next Thursday."

The Crooked Shekel

(The Crooked Man)

There was a crooked man and he had a crooked smile,
He put a crooked shekel right inside the subway 'stile.
The crooked shekel then got stuck inside the crooked slot,
And when he jumped the barrier he crookedly was caught.

Little Tom Krepatke

(Little Tommy Tucker)

Little Tom Krepatke
Sings for 'tato latke.
What puts he on the latke?
Anything you've gotke.

The Queen of Minsk

(The Queen of Hearts)

The Queen of Minsk,
She made a blintz,
All on a winter's eve.
The shnook of Minsk,
He stole the blintz,
And put it up his sleeve.

The Prince of Minsk,
(Who wanted the blintz)
Proclaimed the shnook pernicious.
The shnook of Minsk,
Came forth, and said,
"I found the blintz—delicious!"

Molly and Suzie

(Polly and Sukey)

Molly, put the kreplach on,
Molly, put the kreplach on,
Molly, put the kreplach on,
The guests are coming soon.

Suzie, roll the cabbage up,
Suzie, roll the cabbage up,
Suzie, roll the cabbage up,
We'll save it for next June.

Ring around the Daisies

(Ring around the Roses)

Ring around the daisies!
All my friends are crazies!
Schnorrers! Schnorrers!
We all must plotz!

Oy, Diddle Diddle

(Hey Diddle Diddle)

Oy, diddle diddle!
The cat took his fiddle,
Up onto the roof of his house.
He played Broadway tunes,
By the light of the moon,
And the cow danced with Esther, the mouse.

Jack and Phil

(Jack and Jill)

Jack and Phil went up the hill,
To pitch an ad campaign.
But Phil forsook his Powerbook
And then he went insane.

So Jack and Phil went separate ways
Now Jack's a big-time macher.
And Phil, he's living with nine cats
(We think he's now a stalker.)

Bernie Lee

(Burnie Bee)

Bernie Lee, Bernie Lee
How many will your wedding be?
If it be more than one-fifty,
You'd better invite your cousin Swifty.

Hannukah Is Coming

(Christmas Is Coming)

Hannukah is coming, dust off your menorah!
Get ready to eat latkes (and to maybe dance the hora)!
Buy your presents early to avoid the mishegoss,
Or you'll see all the goys out doing shopping for Christmas.

One, Two I'm Gonna Sue

(One, Two Buckle my Shoe)

One, two I'm gonna sue.
Three, four, fix that floor!
Five, six, do it quick!
Seven, eight, I can't wait.
Nine, ten, I might fall again.
Eleven, twelve, into your past I'll delve.
Thirteen, fourteen, we'll go a-courting.
Fifteen, sixteen, my lawyer's Bernie Brichstein.
Seventeen, eighteen, he's a-waiting.
Nineteen, twenty, he'll get you for plenty.

For Want of a Male

(For Want of a Nail)

For want of a male, I needed a dress.
For want of a dress, I needed a job.
For want of a job, I applied to school.
For want of school, I needed cheap rent.
For want of cheap rent, I moved back home—
And all for the want of a stupid male.

Three Men at the Club

(Three Men in a Tub)

Rub a dub dub, three men at the club.
Just sittin' in armchairs and schmoozin'.
The banker, the shrink,
The guy who sells mink,
They're all eatin' and talkin' and boozin'.

This Little Putz

(This Little Pig)

This little putz went to Walgreens.
This little putz stayed in the car.
This little putz had brisket.
This little putz had none.
And this little putz went oy, oy, oy all the way home.

De Glussary

(Mostly from *The Joys of Yiddish*, by Leo Rosten)

Alter kocker. (n) (AHL-ter KAH-ker) A crotchety old man; an old fart.

Blintz. (n) (blints) A crepe filled with cottage cheese and eaten with jam. Delicious.

Boychik. (n) (BOY-chick) An affectionate term for boy.

Brisket. (n) (BRIS-kit) A beef dish that is cooked for hours, days, or years and served in every good Jewish home.

Bubbi. (n) (BUH-bee) An affectionate term for grandma.

Chazzer. (n) (CHAHZ-zir, with the "ch" as if you're coughing up phlegm.) A cheapskate.

Chutzpah. (n) (CHOOTS-pah, as in "foot-spa" with the "ch" as in "chazzer") Unmitigated gall. The classic example of *chutzpah* is the boy who kills his parents and then asks the court for mercy because he's an orphan.

Dumbkopf. (n) (DOOM-cough) An idiot. From the German, literally "stupid head."

Farchacda. (adj) (fuh-KOCK-duh) Dizzy, confused, stunned, or in pain.

Farmisht. (adj) (fur-MISHED) Confused or mixed up.

Fartoosht. (adj) (fuh-TOOSHED) Bewildered or discombobulated.

Gevalt. (excl) (geh-VAULT) A cry for help, as in "Oy gevalt."

Gebentsht. (adj) (geh-BENCHED) Blessed.

Gefilte. (n) (geh-FILL-tuh) A ball or cake of seasoned, minced fish that looks like part of the brain and is usually eaten on Passover.

Goyim. (n) (GOY-im, as in "boy him") Plural of "goy," or non-Jewish person.

Gonif. (n) (GONE-if) A con artist or trickster.

Hora. (n) (WHORE-a as in "bore a") Jewish folk dance.

Hannukah. (n) (CHAH-new-kuh) The traditional Jewish festival of lights that lasts for eight days and nights in December.

Kishka. (n) (KISH-kuh, as in "wish-kuh") A traditional kosher sausage dish. Also, intestines or entrails.

Klutz. (n) (klutz, as in "huts") A clumsy person or bungler.

Knish. (n) (k-NISH, as in "the wish") A dumpling-like pastry, usually filled with potatoes or chopped liver.

Kreplach. (n) (KREHP-lach, as in "step-lach") A ravioli-like dumpling, usually filled with meat or cheese and served in soup.

Kugel. (n) (KOO-gull) A noodle pudding.

Kvell. (v) (k-VEHLL, as in "well") To gush or speak of or about with immense pride.

Kvetch. (v) (k-VETCH, as in "fetch") To complain.

Latke. (n) (LOT-key) A potato pancake.

Macher. (n) (MOCH-er) A person with lots of connections, an operator.

Mensch. (n) (mentch, as in "bench") A good person, someone to admire.

Meshugge. (adj) (meh-SHU-gey, as in "foot-key") Crazy, nuts.

Mishegoss. (n) (mish-eh-GAWZ) Craziness, chaos.

Nudnik. (n) (NUD-nick, as in "foot-nick") An annoying person, a bore.

Oy. (excl) (oy, as in "boy") My goodness!

Oy vay iz meer. (excl) (oy-vayz-MEER) Literally, "Oh woe is me."

Passover. (n) Jewish holiday celebrating the exodus of the Jews from Egypt.

Peckel. (n) (PECK-uhl, as in "freckle") A little package.

Pisher. (n) (PISH-er, as in "fisher") A nobody.

Plotz. (v) (plots) To burst or collapse.

Pupik. (n) (PU-pick, as in "foot pick") Bellybutton.

Putz. (n) (putts) A fool. Also, the male genitalia.

Schnorrer. (n) (SHNORE-er, as in "horror") A bum or a drifter.

Shabbat. (n) (shuh-BAHT, as in "the cot") The Jewish Sabbath, which runs from sundown on Friday to sundown on Saturday.

Shekel. (n) (SHEH-kuhl, as in "heckle") A coin, literally the most important silver coin in biblical times.

Shiksa. (n) (SHICK-suh, as in "flicksa") A non-Jewish woman.

Shlemeil. (n) (shluh-MEEL, as in "the peel") A fool or loser.

Schmooze. (v) (shmooz) To converse.

Shnecken. (n) (SHNEH-kin, as in "fleck in") A little pastry.

Shnook. (n) (shnook, as in "book") A sad sack, a loser.

Shpeil. (n) (shpeel) To converse, or chit-chat.

Shul. (n) (shool, as in "cool") Synagogue.

Traif. (adj) (trayf, as in "waif") Unkosher.

Tucchis/Tushie. (n) (TUCH-iss/TUSH-ee, as in "bush key") Rear end.